D0119492

A catalogue record for this book is available from the British Library

Published by Ladybird Books Ltd
80 Strand London WC2R 0RL
A Penguin Company

2 4 6 8 10 9 7 5 3 1

Shoes and Hats

Ladybird

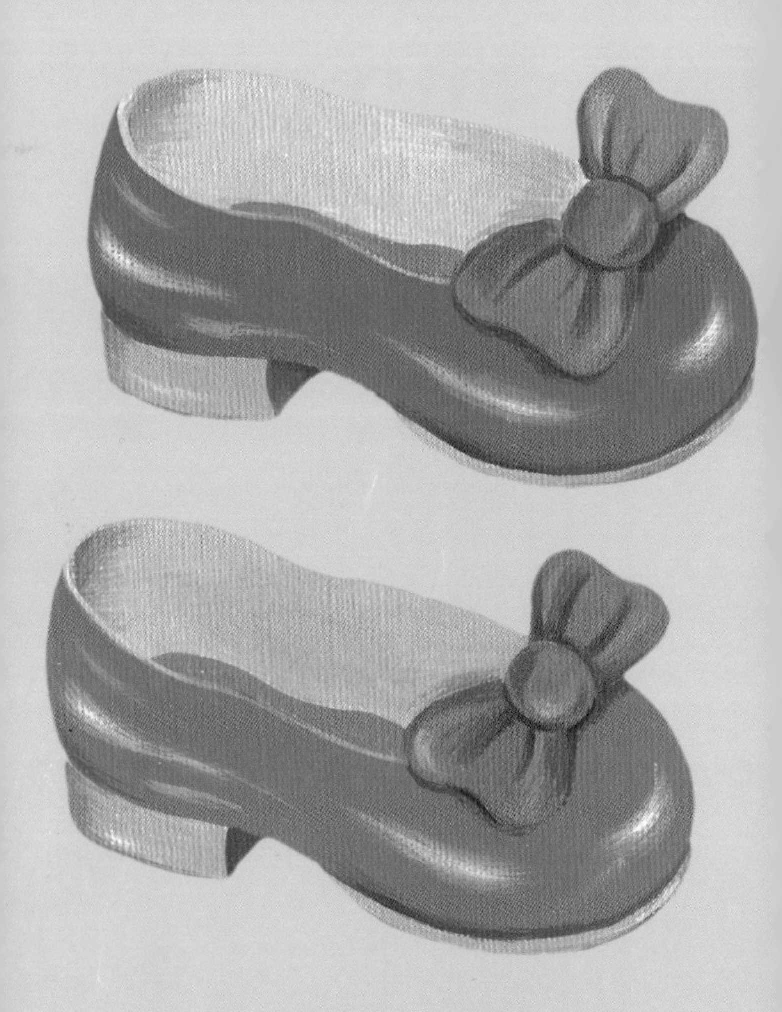

shiny shoes

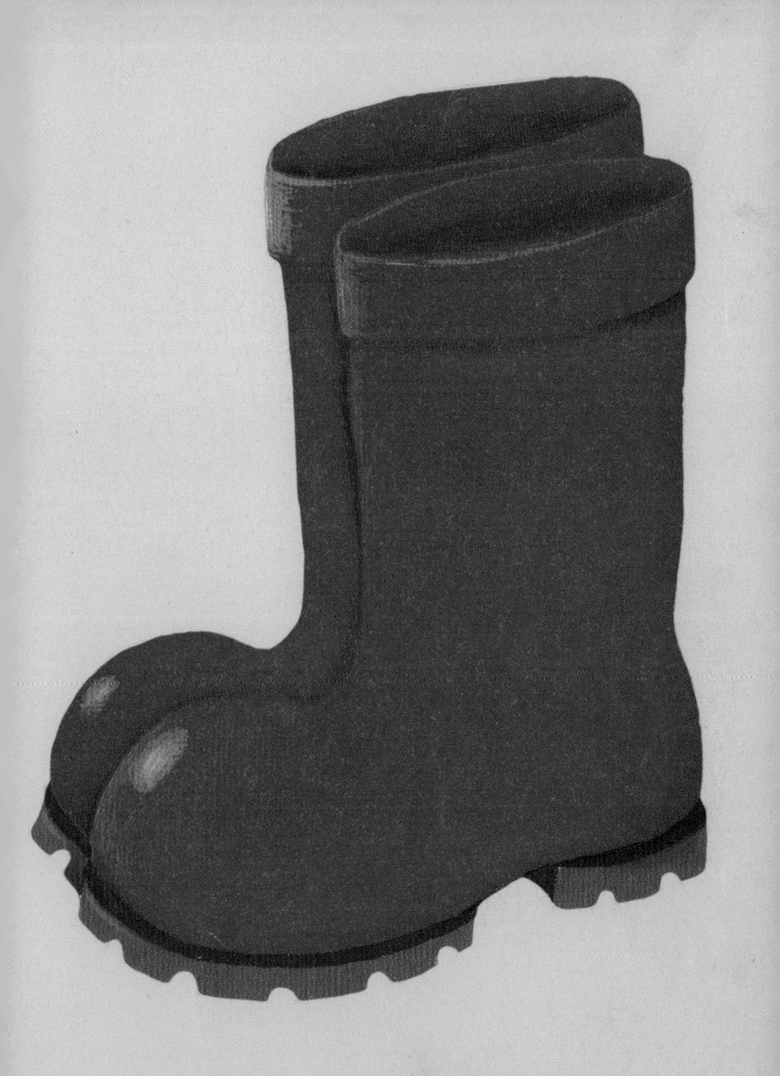

rubber boots

woolly sweater

bobble hat

purple t-shirt

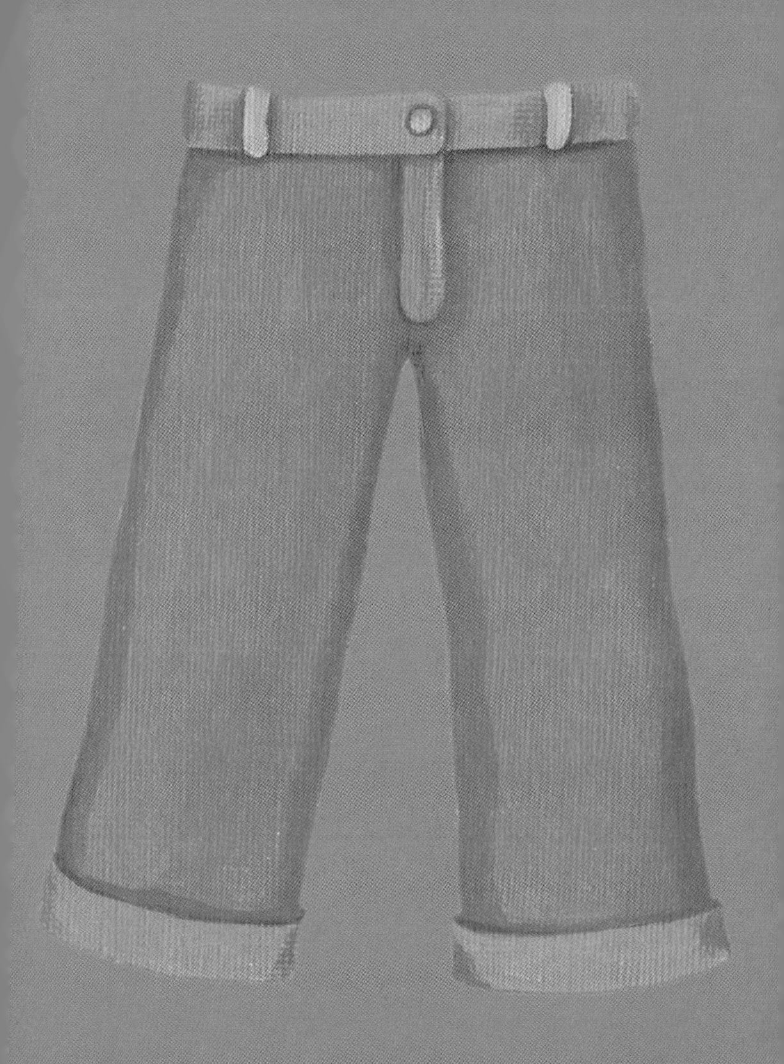

orange trousers

green bikini

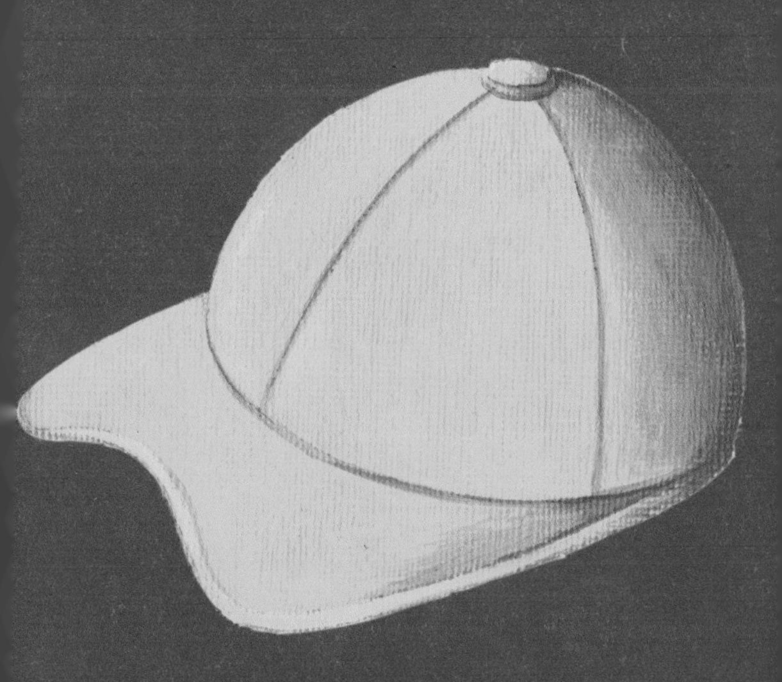

yellow cap

summer sandals

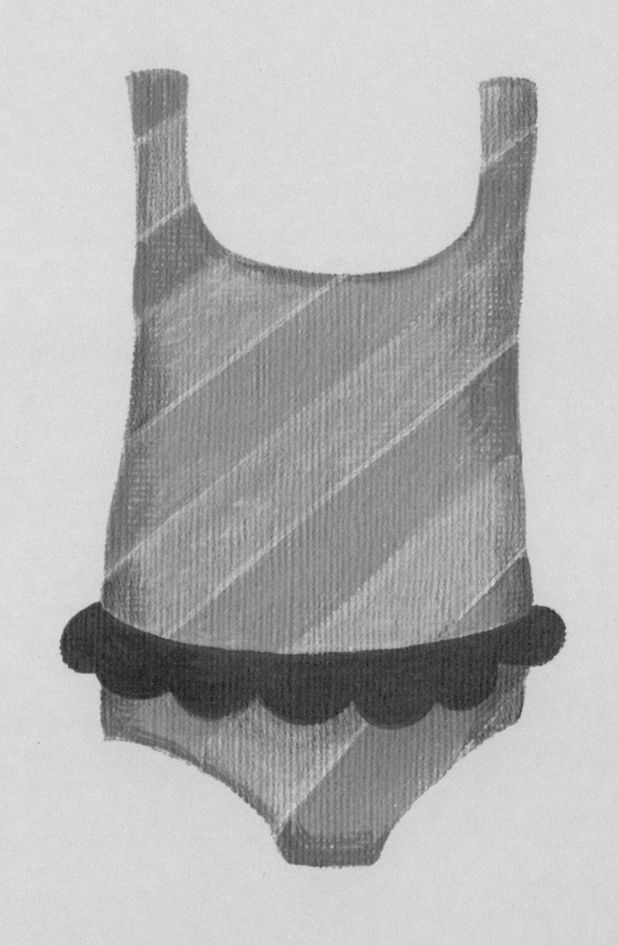

stripy swimsuit

flowery skirt

cotton vest

sparkly shoes

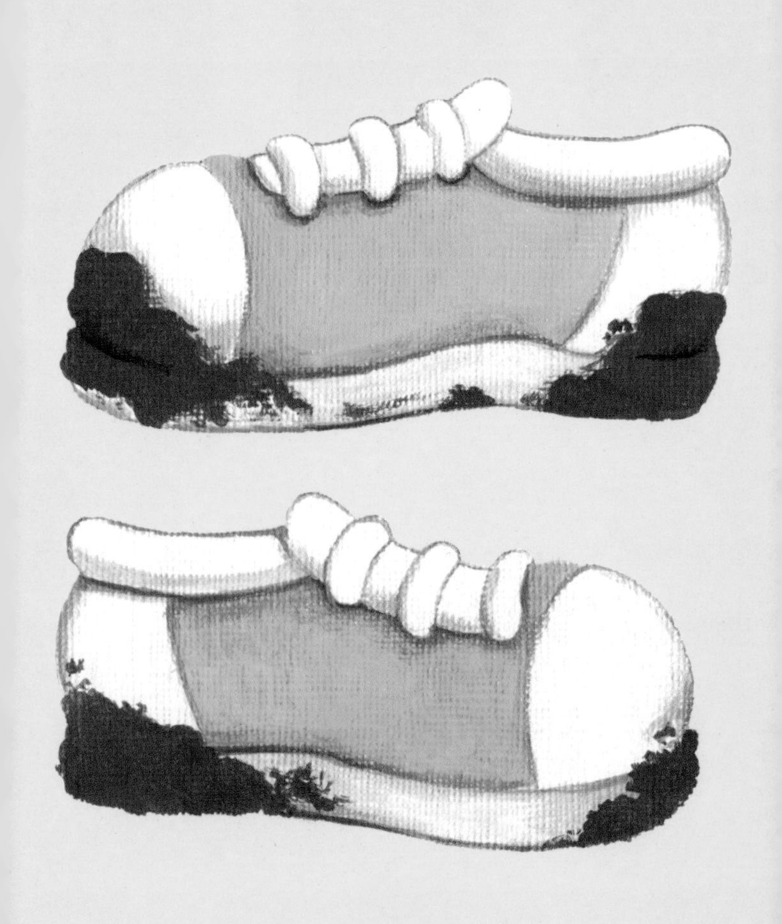

muddy trainers

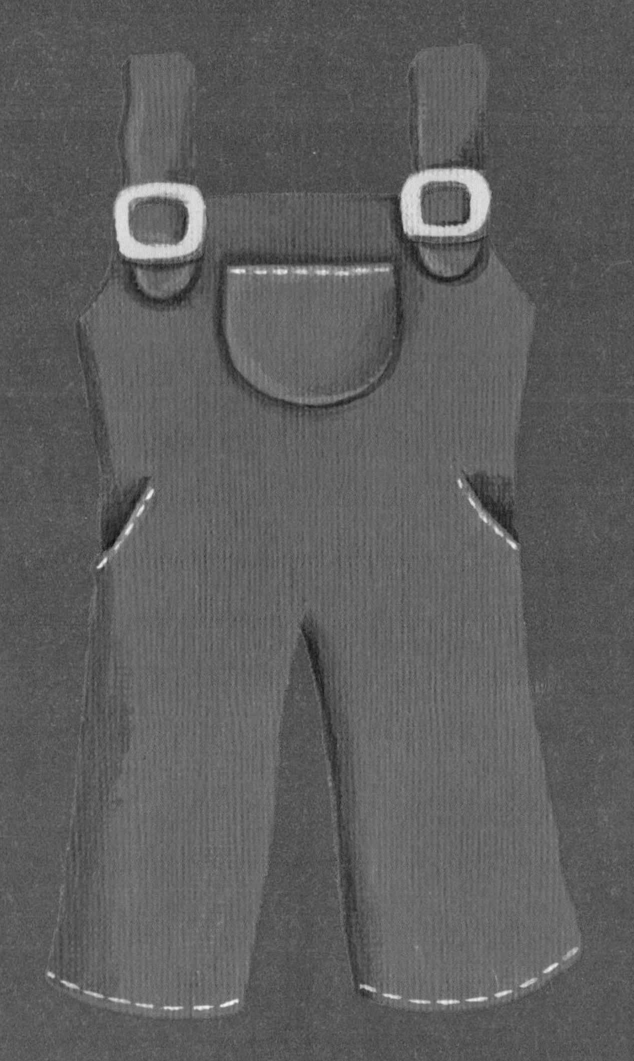

blue dungarees

party dress

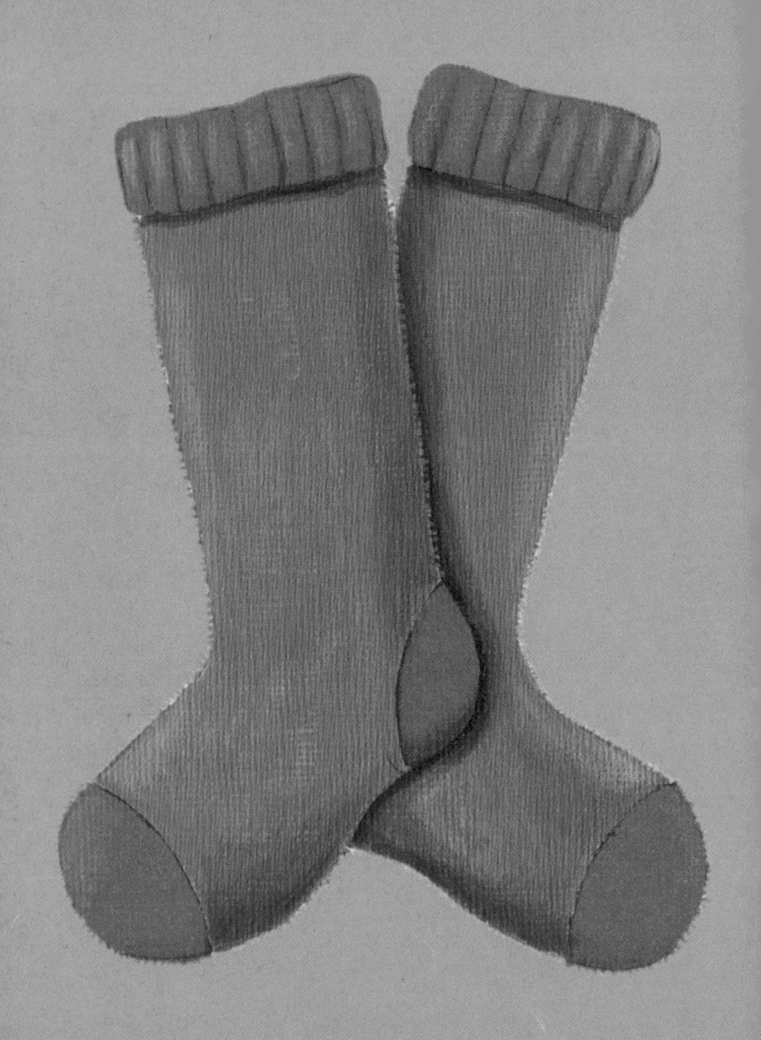

stretchy socks

soft cardigan

spotty nightdress

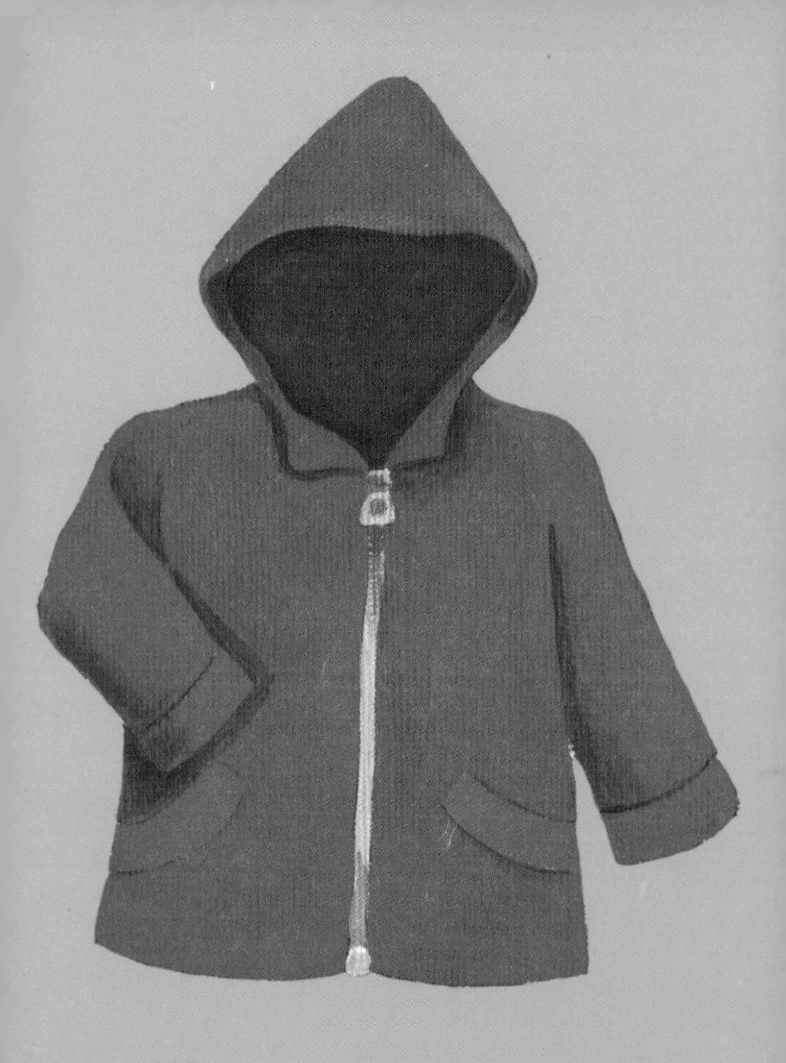

red raincoat

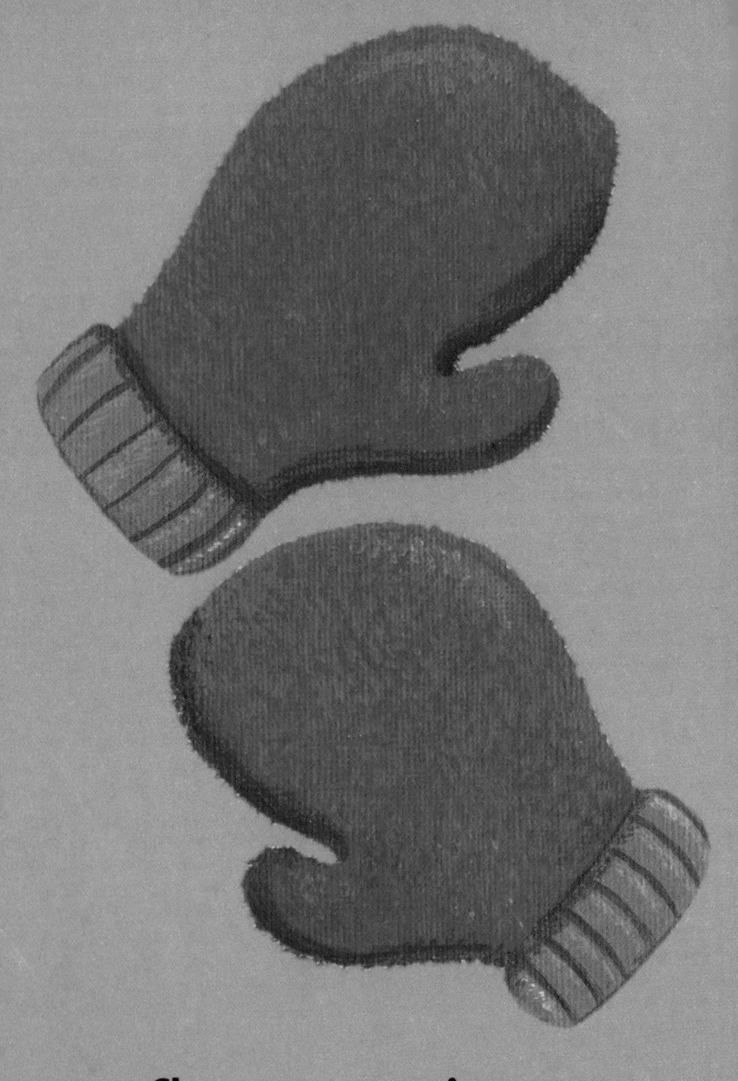

fleecy mittens

bunny slippers

pink pyjamas

sun hat